THE WISHING SEED

Lily the Elf

Kane Miller
A DIVISION OF EDC PUBLISHING

Kane Miller, A Division of EDC Publishing

For information contact:
Kane Miller, A Division of EDC Publishing
PO Box 470663
Tulsa, OK 74147-0663
www.kanemiller.com
www.edcpub.com
www.usbornebooksandmore.com

Library of Congress Control Number: 2015957640
Printed and bound in the United States of America
1 2 3 4 5 6 7 8 9 10
ISBN: 978-1-61067-531-4

THE WISHING SEED

Lily the Elf

Anna Branford

Illustrated by Lisa Coutts

 Chapter one

Lily lives with her dad
in a tiny elf house,
hidden under a bridge
in a busy city.

In the moss garden behind the house there is an even tinier house called a granny flat. And in the granny flat lives Lily's granny.

Lily is lying in the moss garden reading a book. The book is about an elf princess. It is Lily's favorite.

She likes the princess's crown best. It is covered in sparkles.

Lily wishes she had a
real elf princess crown.
The crown she's wearing is
just for dress up. (And one
of the points is broken.)

Suddenly, something
fluffy floats over the
garden. It's a dandelion
seed! Lily jumps up.
Dandelion seeds
are lucky.

If she catches
one, she'll get to
make a wish.

Lily stretches up. The wishing seed is just out of reach. She leaps and hops, but not quite high enough. She scrambles up onto a rock. She stands on her tippiest toes. But it is no good. The dandelion seed starts to drift away.

Lily has another idea.
She squats down very
low on the rock. Then
she springs into the air.

It is the highest she has ever jumped. She is just in time to catch the dandelion seed!

Lily's dress up crown falls off her head. (Now another point is broken.) She knows exactly what to wish for.

Chapter two

Lily hugs the seed tightly. Then she whispers into the fluff.

Lovely dandelion seed
(not a pest and not a weed),
grant my wish
with super speed,
a princess crown
is what I need!

She holds the seed just
a moment longer. Then
she sets it free again.
She watches it sail
away on the soft breeze.

Lily runs into the
kitchen. Dad is having a
cup of tea.

"I'm getting an elf
princess crown!" Lily tells
him.

"That sounds exciting," says Dad. "How do you know?"

"Because I wished on a dandelion seed," explains Lily.

"But dandelion seed wishes don't always come true," says Dad. (Lily knew Dad would say that.)

"This one will," says Lily.

Lily goes back outside.
Granny is watering the
flowers by her window.

"I'm getting an elf
princess crown!" Lily tells
her.

"How wonderful," says Granny. "Where from?"

"I don't know," admits Lily. She is hopping in the moss with excitement. "I wished on a dandelion seed. I even gave it a hug!"

"I've always found that fixing things works better than wishing for them," says Granny. (Lily guessed Granny would say that.)

"But wishing is much more fun than fixing," says Lily.

Lily goes into her room and gets out her pencils and paper.

She draws a picture of herself wearing her new crown. It is fun adding the sparkles.

Lily waits patiently for her new elf princess crown to arrive.

 Chapter three

All day, Lily watches
the sparrows carefully.
Perhaps one will swoop
down with her crown in

its beak. She also looks out for dragonflies. Maybe one will fly over and drop her crown right onto her head. In the evening, she keeps the window open. A mail bee might buzz by with a special late delivery.

After dinner and a bath,
Lily puts on her pajamas.
The elf princess crown
has not arrived. Lily
starts to worry.

I said super speed,
she thinks. *But this is
not super speed. It is not
even normal speed.
This is snail speed.*

"Are you all right,
Lily?" asks Dad. He has

come to say good night.
"My crown wish still
hasn't come true," says
Lily, frowning.

"Sometimes that's the way with dandelion seeds," says Dad.

"Is something wrong, Lily?" asks Granny. She has come to tuck Lily in.

"My crown wish still hasn't worked," says Lily, huffing.

"Sometimes that's the way with wishes," says Granny.

"But this wish was a special one," says Lily. "And I still only have a silly old, broken crown."

"And a beautiful drawing," says Dad.

Dad and Granny look
at the picture Lily drew.

"I like all the sparkles,"
says Granny, looking at
the crown.

"That's the elf princess
crown I wished for," says
Lily.

Lily doesn't feel like
frowning and huffing
anymore. She sniffles
sadly into her pillow.

# Chapter four

In the morning, Lily searches the garden. An ant might have delivered her elf princess crown

overnight. But she only
finds one of the points of
her old crown.

"What's that?" asks Dad. He has brought some breakfast outside.

"Just a broken bit of crown," says Lily.

"I bet I can fix it for you," says Dad.

"I only have one of the missing points," Lily reminds him.

"I'll see what I can do," says Dad.

After breakfast Dad
glues the point back onto
the crown. Then he looks
in his box of useful things.

Lily is only half watching. She is waiting for the mail bee. Just in case.

Dad finds some pieces of gold wire. He bends them into points. Then he glues them onto the crown.

"How's that?" he asks Lily, showing her.

The wires don't quite match.

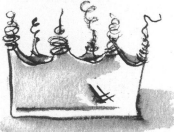

"A bit better. Thanks, Dad," says Lily.

Granny comes over to have a look too.

"The new points aren't quite right," says Granny. "I think I know a way to make them look better."

"Okay. Thanks, Granny," says Lily. She is only half listening. She is still looking out for the  mail bee.

Granny takes the crown into her house.

The mail bee comes.
He does not bring
anything
for Lily.
Lily flops
sadly in
the moss.
Maybe
Dad and
Granny were
right about
dandelion seed wishes.

But even though she is very sad, Lily notices something. Interesting noises are coming out of the granny flat.

 Chapter five

First Lily hears some clunking. Then some rummaging. Then some rustling. She goes over to

the granny flat to see what
Granny is doing.

The crown is resting
on some old elf
newspaper. Granny
has been painting it.
Now all the points are
different colors.

"That looks much
better!" says Lily. She
walks around it slowly.

"Yes," agrees Granny.

"But I think it needs something else too."

Lily looks in one of Granny's old suitcases. It is full of things the humans have left behind.

"How about this?" Lily holds up a green glass bead.

"Good idea,"
says Granny.

Next Lily finds
a silver star.

"How about this?"

"Even better!" says
Granny.

"And this?" asks Lily.
She holds up a tiny gold
flower that was once part
of a human earring.

"Perfect!" says Granny.

Before too long Lily has made a pile of sparkles. Granny helps her to glue one onto each point of her crown.

When the glue is dry, Lily tries it on.

"How do I look?"

"Like an elf princess," says Granny.

Lily runs out to show Dad.

"What do you think?" she asks.

"I think," says Dad, "that your wish might have come true after all."

Lily looks at the crown in her book. Then she looks at the crown in her drawing. Then she looks at herself, reflected

in a puddle. She has the
most beautiful elf princess
crown of all.

Other
Lily the Elf
books by
**Anna
Branford**

Lily the elf finds a
beautiful ring.

The midnight owl
sounds scary!

Lily the elf has a
brand-new elf flute.